**As seen in

TUESDAY

WARNING:
May contain
traces of:
· bad hair
· lucky undies
· **KABOOMS.**

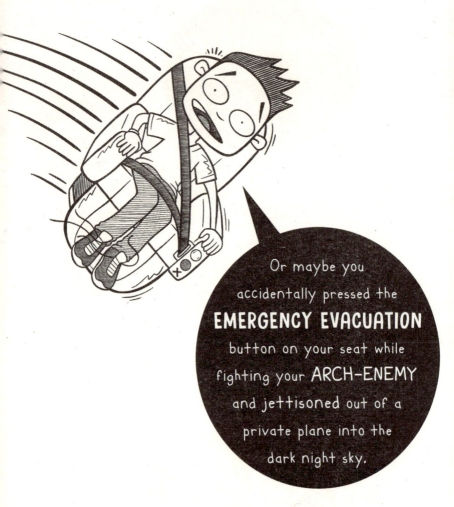

*As seen in **MONDAY**

WARNING:
May contain traces of:
· slime
· spew
· possible alien abductions.

OK. SO THIS ISN'T A BAD WEEK.

IT'S THE ...

WORST WEEK EVER!

Monday was MESSY! Tuesday was TERRIBLE!

NOW WELCOME TO ...

For Mum & Dad

First published in Great Britain in 2023 by Simon & Schuster UK Ltd

First published in Australia in 2022 by Scholastic Australia
An imprint of Scholastic Australia Pty Limited
PO Box 579 Gosford NSW 2250

1 3 5 7 9 10 8 6 4 2

Simon & Schuster UK Ltd
1st Floor, 222 Gray's Inn Road
London
WC1X 8HB

www.simonandschuster.co.uk
www.simonandschuster.com.au
www.simonandschuster.co.in

Simon & Schuster India, New Delhi

A CIP catalogue record for this book is available from the British Library.

PB ISBN 978-1-3985-2197-1
eBook ISBN 978-1-3985-2198-8

Typeset in Adorkable, Harimau, Kiddish, Sugary Pancake and Zakka.

Printed and Bound in the UK using 100% Renewable Electricity
at CPI Group (UK) Ltd

MIX
Paper | Supporting
responsible forestry
FSC® C171272
FSC
www.fsc.org

EVA AMORES & MATT COSGROVE

...WEDNESDAY

Simon & Schuster

LET'S JUMP IN HERE!

6:27am

'WAKE UP!'

My eyelids spring wide open. My pupils dart around in a panic. An endless expanse of blue sky fills my view and I remember **exactly** where I am. I slam my eyes closed again.

'WAKE UP, POO BOY!'

No. No. No. **No. NO!** I scrunch my eyelids tighter, trying to block out the light and the truth. But there's no escaping the **horrible** reality of my current, **TRAGIC** situation.

... in the middle of **who-knows-where ocean** ...

COLOUR
BY
NUMBER

2 = BLUE

2

Yes, this is an
entirely giant
Number 2 situation!

Of **ALL** the people on the planet, Marvin would **literally** be the **LAST** person I would ever pick to be stuck in a raft with.

CHOOSE YOUR CREWMATE

MUM

SKILLS: Martial arts, medical knowledge, great HUGS, laser eyes, TOUGH!

She would give me a hug and know what to do.

DAD

PULL MY FINGER!

PROS: Inventive, resourceful, optimistic. CONS: Farts. A LOT!

He would make me laugh.

MIA

PROS: Kind, creative, brave. CONS: None. (Except she's seen me in my lucky undies!)

I could use a real friend right now!

NAN

#@&*!!

SKILLS: Storytelling, crocheting, tea-drinking, wisdom of experience.

I'd learn some new swear words for sure!

14

CAPTAIN FLUFFYKINS

HISS

SKILLS: Scratching, death-staring, scratching, sleeping, scratching.

Let's face it, he would probably intentionally puncture the raft, but I really miss him!

WOLF GRUNTZ

GRRRRR!

PROS: Ex-military, highly skilled, unkillable, legend.
CONS: Very intimidating.

Celebrity survival expert from my fave show *DUDE VS DEATH* would save the day.

NICKERS

WOOF!

SKILLS: Tail-wagging, stealing, drooling, barking, licking.

She's always so happy to see me! Good for raft morale.

MARVIN

PROS: Absolutely none!
CONS: Absolutely EVERYTHING!!

Never, never, ever! Not this guy. Please, NO! It's almost as though sinister outside forces are controlling my life for their own personal twisted entertainment.

Marvin is shaking me, but I realise his whole body is **shaking** too. His usual **icy** glare has been replaced by wide-eyed **FEAR**.

YESTERDAY   TODAY

'WAKE UP! WAKE UP! WAKE UP!' Marvin splutters.
'I'm awake. I'M AWAKE! **I'M AWAKE!**' I assure him.
'Shhh ... Shhh ... Shhh ...' he's stammering.
'Now you're **SHUSHING** me?!'

Marvin shakes his head and points out to the ocean.
I follow the direction of his **trembling** finger. And then I see it. **Slicing** through the water. Headed straight for us.

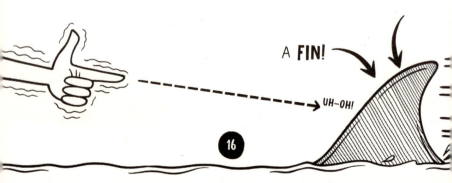

A **FIN!**

UH-OH!

Correction ...

'SHARKS!'

How did I get myself into **THIS SITUATION?**

That's a **VERY** good question. I'm glad you asked. Let's **review** the footage.

SITUATION CHECKLIST

☑ INFLATABLE RAFT

☑ MIDDLE OF THE OCEAN

☑ SWORN ENEMY

☑ SURROUNDED BY SHARKS

⏪ REWIND

I DID A POO POO! I'M A BIG BOY.

Not **THAT** far back! I meant just last night. When I accidentally **ejected** from the plane ...

LAST NIGHT

So my parachute has deployed, I'm casually minding my own business, gliding down towards an unknown but certainly **terrible** fate and then ...

INCOMING!

SLOW MOTION

... I cop a

FACE FULL OF

FEET!

Super expensive and impossibly clean sneakers!

SERIOUSLY?

I actually **eject** midair from a plane and I **STILL** can't escape the guy who is deliberately **ruining** my life!

FREEZE FRAME

OOOPPHHH!

21

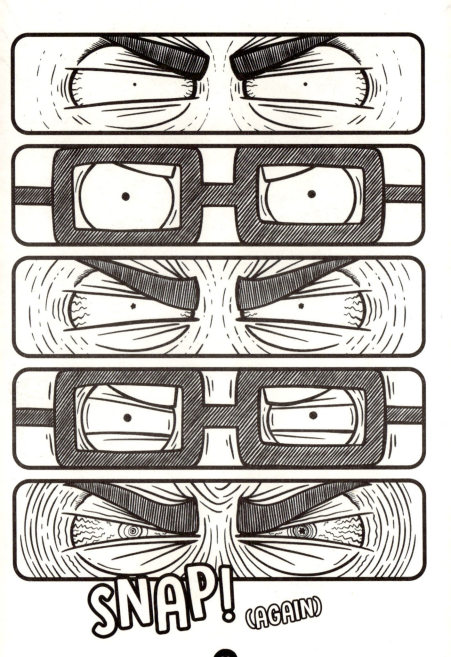

Fighting whilst parachuting is actually **much** harder than it looks! Despite our best efforts, and some serious **TRASH TALKING** (sorry, Mum!), our aerial altercation doesn't achieve much.

We're so engrossed in our sky-high **SKIRMISH**, we don't even notice that we are **RAPIDLY** running out of sky until ...

We **HIT** the water, then everything happens in a **BLUR**.

The impact triggers the life raft stowed within my seat to pop out.

POP!

My parachute disconnects and blows off into the darkness.

PPFSH!

My seatbelt springs open.

CLICK!

Now it cooperates! Typical!

I paddle across to my life raft, which has automatically inflated, and climb inside. There's a life jacket and survival kit. I'm **SAFE!**

I peer over the edge to look for Marvin. His emergency raft **hasn't** inflated. It's floating on the water's surface, **SHRIVELLED** up like one of Dad's famous fried eggs (before his **GROSS GREEN DIET**).

QUITE GOOD

Extra crispy

QUITE BAD

Extra cruddy

I spot Marvin, his arms **FLAILING** wildly, bobbing beneath the waves and **GASPING** for air. Our eyes lock.

I ... (GLUB) CAN'T ... (SPLUTTER) SWIM!

I **CAN** swim. I have the laminated certificates and a temporarily misplaced box of trophies to prove it!

So shiny

Without thinking, I dive into the water and grab Marvin, dragging him over to my raft. That's the **EASY** part. Getting him **INTO** the raft is the hard part.

It's a **STRUGGLE!**
After a few failed
attempts, I eventually
manage to hoist Marvin
up into the life boat.

It might have
involved giving him a
major **WEDGIE,** but
I had to do what I had
to do. Promise I didn't
enjoy doing it! (Much.)

We both flop, completely **EXHAUSTED,** onto the bouncy
floor of the life boat and try to catch our breath.

After the **FRENZY** of action, it's now very still and quiet. The lightning storm has eased and the **DARKNESS** of the night surrounds us. Marvin has put on the one life vest, but the survival kit has been lost overboard. I'm suddenly feeling the seriousness of our situation **BIG TIME!**

I'm a few shallow breaths away from full **MELTDOWN** mode when Marvin softly speaks, breaking the silence.

I wasn't expecting that. At all. It **JOLTS** me out of my panic spiral. I don't know what to reply, but Marvin keeps talking in the same hushed tone.

'And I'm sorry for being ... well ... being a bully.'

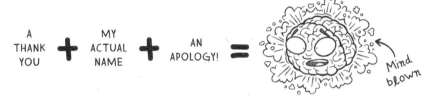

A THANK YOU **+** MY ACTUAL NAME **+** AN APOLOGY! **=** Mind blown

Marvin is being nice and it doesn't seem like an act for once! Did we land in an alternate parallel universe? Is this **Opposite Land** – or Ocean to be technical. Are we in the Bermuda Triangle? Wherever that is! I'm not sure, because I kind of tune out whenever Dad starts ranting about it. And, boy, does he love to **RANT** about it.

I glance over at Marvin. I don't see the slick, sneaky **BULLY** right now. I see a regular kid, just like me, **shivering** and SCARED.

THEN   **NOW**

'Why *were* you so mean to me?' The question just pops out, but I genuinely want to know the answer.

Marvin shrugs and sighs. 'Do you know what it's like to be the school principal's son? The **WORST!** I used to get teased, picked on and called names ALL the time.'

FLASHBACK WITHIN A FLASHBACK

'Until I realised I could change the **target** to someone else. The weird kid. The different kid. The new kid. Anyone but me. It was easy. And then I just kind of kept doing it.'

I'm not sure it's a great reason, or even a valid excuse, but it seems like an HONEST answer at least.

'Can I ask you another question?'

Marvin nods.

'Are you wearing Hoppy Doppy undies?'

Marvin turns bright red.

'They're my **LUCKY UNDIES!**' he blurts out.

'You're currently stranded in a glorified **pool floatie** in the middle of nowhere in the dead of night with me! I think we can officially rule out how lucky those undies are, Marvin.'

We both **giggle** a little bit.

For some reason, I start to hum *If You're Hoppy and You Know It*. And I feel marginally better. Marvin slowly joins in, and the humming gradually morphs into **mumbling** the lyrics, until eventually we're both SINGING the song at the top of our lungs.

At the end of the final chorus we both burst out LAUGHING uncontrollably.

'That song is a **CLASSIC!**' Marvin declares.

'That's what I always say!' I laugh. 'And Cloppy Doppy is the **best!**' I continue with the Hoppy Doppy fan-boying.

Marvin abruptly stops laughing. His eyebrows are furrowed. His eyes cold. 'You're not serious, are you? Floppy Doppy is CLEARLY the greatest of all time.'

'Cloppy Doppy has ALL the brains!'

'Floppy Doppy has ALL the talent.'

Team CLOPPY

Team Floppy

'Cloppy Doppy!'
'Floppy Doppy!'
'CLOPPY DOPPY!'
'FLOPPY DOPPY!'
'CLOPPY. DOPPY!'
'FLOPPY **FULL STOP** DOPPY **EXCLAMATION MARK!**'
'**C** to the **L** to the **O** to the **P** to the **P** to the **Y** DOPPY!'
'Capital **F** to the capital **L** to the capital **O** to the
capital **P** to the capital **P** to the capital **Y** to the power of
INFINITY times one hundred DOPPY!'

And then we're fighting again, kicking and scratching
over the best Hoppy Doppy ...

... until we collapse from exhaustion once more.

Poor
Sloppy
Doppy

I turn my back to Marvin, who has now well and truly returned to the **TOP SPOT** on my **Complete and Utter Pain in the Neck List**, and I squeeze my eyes tightly closed.

I know there must be whole rescue teams desperately **searching** for us right now and any second we'll be **SAVED**. I just need to hold on, stay calm and be patient.

Time to find **MY HAPPY PLACE™** in my head.

I imagine the warmth of Mum's **HUG** as her arms wrap around me.

I imagine Dad clutching his jiggling stomach, laughing as I point out you can rearrange the letters in **RAFT** to spell **FART**.

I imagine holding Captain Fluffykins – back when he used to be **CUTE**.

And **somehow** I drift off to sleep.

Relief washes over me. I'm **NOT** going to be featured in an upcoming, **gory** re-enactment scene in a **SHARK WEEK** nature documentary! PHEW!

VOICEOVER (whispered in posh accent):

'At this point, Nature's perfect killing machine devours the hapless human interlopers as though they are chicken nuggets at an all-you-can-eat buffet.'

Grainy black and white footage for extra drama

Why is the actor playing Marvin so much better looking than the actor playing me?!

Despite Dad's evil marine overlord conspiracy theories*, these dolphins seem very **FRIENDLY.** They dart and dive around the raft, occasionally **leaping** into the air in joyous arcs. Then they surround us in formation, lining their bodies up against the sides of the raft. The dolphins **CLICK** in unison and then swim, full speed ahead.

*See *Worst Week Ever: Monday* page 37

6:35am

Forget horse-powered.

We're **DOLPHIN-POWERED!**

We glide over the waves at an **exhilarating** speed. The air is rushing through my hair. I feel the mist of water spray **TINGLING** my cheeks. I'm cheering in sheer **delight!**

And then, on the horizon, I see it ... **'LAND?'**

We get closer and it becomes clearer ...**'ISLAND!'**

Closer still and it comes into focus ... **'SCARY SKULL ISLAND!'**

Maybe not ideal, but we're in no position to be choosy.

As we approach the shore, the water gets **CHOPPIER** as the waves begin to **BREAK**. The dolphins **abandon** us and, with a wave of their flippers, return out to sea.

CLICK!* CLICK!** CLICK!***

* You're on your own now, suckers!
** Soon we will return and overthrow your species.
*** Just kidding! Take care.

Our raft is bouncing **WILDLY** on the rough water as the surf pushes us towards the beach. And then ...

CRASH!

... a **MONSTER** wave smashes down, flinging me out of the boat and **dumping** me under the surface in a battering **SWIRL** of surging foam and bubbles.

I **SPIRAL** around in whirling cartwheels, not sure which way is up or down. Just like that time Captain Fluffykins accidentally went for a **SPIN** in the washing machine when he fell asleep in the laundry basket. He was **NOT** happy about that unexpected ride, and now I understand **exactly** why!

THE SPIN CYCLE

Cat nap

Soggy moggy

Eventually, COUGHING and **spluttering**, I'm swept up on the beach right next to Marvin – who seems to have made it ashore more smoothly than me.

It's such a relief to be back on land, I don't even care about Marvin's **snide** comment. I pluck the seaweed and starfish off and stand up to look around for signs of life.

We're on a sandy peninsula that juts out into the ocean like a crooked finger. It seems quite **DESERTED**, though.

It looks like last night's storm has left the shore littered with washed up **DEBRIS**, including one of the plane ejector seats. I take a step towards it and realise there's **SAND** in my shoes and socks. I can feel it **squishing** up between my toes. I take them off and empty them out.

Now I'm aware of all the sand in my jeans. Each step I take **CHAFES** my thighs like there's sandpaper wrapped around my legs.

I try to unload the sand through the leg holes but it's so S L O W !

Like sand through an hourglass.

42

There's no-one around (except Marvin and he doesn't count!), so I quickly whip my jeans off so I can **SHAKE** them out. At this point it becomes pretty obvious there's sand in my **UNDIES** too! It's like a **sand pit** in there. Seriously, I could build a sand castle with the contents. I admit it doesn't look good!

It's not what it looks like, I swear!

'Did you have another accident, Poo Boy?' Marvin laughs. The nice, relatable Marvin from last night in the raft is gone. The old, **MEAN** Marvin is definitely back.

GOODBYE

HELLO AGAIN

I ignore him as I try to deal with the sand situation, but it is literally EVERYWHERE!

In 70 years' time I think I'll **STILL** be finding sand!

FLASH FORWARD

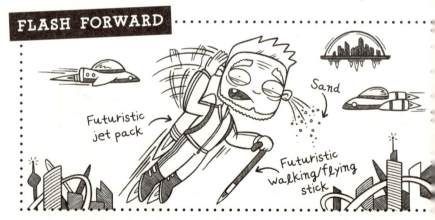

I'm busy washing the never-ending sand out of my clothes at the water's edge when a **sudden** movement catches my eye.

One of the many little shells scattered along the shoreline has sprouted legs and is slowly **SCAMPERING** towards me.

AAARRRGGGHHH!

No, it's **NOT** a cute little crab. It's a cranky crab with **VERY** strong, sharp claws! The pincers **clamp** down painfully on my pointer finger.

I shake my hand in **AGONY** (which probably looks like Dad's 'wave your arms in the air like you just don't care' dance move), sending the crabby crab **FLYING**.

AVENGE ME, BROTHERS!

SPOT THE DIFFERENCE!

Dad's one good shirt →

→ Mystery stain

OWW!

Now I've woken up the whole shell neighbourhood. Suddenly, I'm surrounded by crabs **SCUTTLING** towards me, apparently seeking **REVENGE**. I'm outnumbered and scared.

SNAP SNAP SNAP SNAP SNAP

Dad might need to add **THE CRAB ATTACK** to his dance repertoire, because I am going off right now!

As I flick off the final crab, I look over at Marvin, who seems to be filming my crustacean **CRISIS** on his **TABLET!**

'Where did you get **that?!**' I exclaim.

'I just found it, tucked in my plane seat pocket. Luckily it has a waterproof case. I like to edit my videos in the bath.'

'Now, can you do the crab thing again? I missed the first bit. And ... **ACTION!**'

'Stop recording and call for **HELP!**' I scream at him.

'I already tried. **OBVIOUSLY**. But there's no reception at all. So I might as well get some **quality content** for my channel,' Marvin says matter-of-factly.

'CRAB BOY is the new **POO BOY**. I'm going to get so many views on this!'

'Is that ALL you can think about?!' I yell.

'Calm your farm, Crab Boy! Here are the facts ...'

THE FACTS ACCORDING TO MARVIN KING

1. Everyone on the planet will be looking for us right now.
2. They will find us very soon.
3. I will be hailed a hero for ejecting out of the plane to save you, aka Poo Boy.
4. My incredible bravery and subsequent story of survival will inspire the world.
5. I will be internationally famous.

Continues...

6. My mum will realise she doesn't love your dad, publicly dump him and I will never see you ever again, except for video replays on my number one channel.

7. There will be merchandise. SO much merch!

Free shipping on orders over £50

Marvin smiles **smugly**. 'Now do the crab thing again.'
I throw a **CLUMP** of wet sand right at him.

WHOOSSSHHH!

I miss. By **MILES**.

'Fine. I don't need you,' Marvin decides. He turns his tablet to selfie mode and starts recording ...

MARVELOUS MARVIN
Video Diary DAY 1

TRANSCRIPT:

Hello, world. Is anyone there? It's Marvin here, from the MARVELOUS MARVIN channel. Like and subscribe! Fear not, loyal followers. I am still alive. JUST. No thanks to Poo Boy.

My bravery has already saved us from certain demise in the turbulent skies and savage seas. And now we appear to be stranded on a deserted island. No sign of civilization.

Some call me a HERO. And who am I to disagree ...

I can't stand listening to Marvin's nauseating ramble anymore, so I wander off. Help is **hopefully** on the way, but I feel like I should do something, **ANYTHING**, in the meantime.

I wrack my brain trying to recall the island episodes of my all-time favourite TV show.

Mum and I **never** miss it! Each week, extreme adventurer, ex-military tough guy **WOLF GRUNTZ**, gets air-dropped into a new **NIGHTMARE** scenario. Then he has to make it out **alive** purely on his wits and skills.

What would Wolf Gruntz do in this situation?

Well, he'd probably drink his own **PEE**. He's always drinking his own pee. He's mad for it. Can't get enough.

I'm definitely not up to the 'drink your own urine' desperation stage yet. Maybe something a little less **EXTREME?** Like the classic rescue signal!

I decide I'll make a giant **S.O.S.** sign on the beach so the search parties can spot us easily from the sky. I can't really remember exactly what the letters **S.O.S.** stand for, though.

While I go about arranging the rocks and shells, I try to come up with possible **ACRONYM** answers.

WHAT DOES S.O.S. EVEN STAND FOR?

Smelly
Odd
Socks

Skunk
On
Skates

Scary
Otter
Skeleton

Stinky
Onion
Sandwiches

Create
your
own!

Snivelling
Obnoxious
Slimeball

Speaking of Marvin, he's dragged over the ejector seat and is just watching me work away. He's reclining, like a **KING** on his throne, making annoying, judgy comments.

IN REALITY   ## IN HIS HEAD

'One **S** is slightly bigger than the other **S!**' Marvin notes.

'You could **ACTUALLY** help!' I seeth.

'I **could**. But I **WON'T.** Manual labour is not really my scene. I'm more of an artist, full of ideas and creativity.'

'You're full of **SOMETHING,** all right!'

'And you're so **tetchy.** Maybe a song will cheer you up? You've made the perfect backdrop for my performance.'

And then he begins singing and re-enacting the video clip of Justin Chase's power ballad/pirate rap hit single **'S.O.S.'**.

S.O.S. by Justin Chase

You shipwrecked my heart
On this island of pain.
Then you buried my heart,
How will I find it again?

S.O.S.!
I need to profess.
So. Oh. Sorry.
That I'm in this mess.

(Pirate Rap Time)
Ahoy there, me hearties.
X marks the spot.
I dig you. I dig you.
I dig you a lot.
Head north. Turn east.
Go south. Then west.
Find the key to my heart
In my (treasure) chest.
S.O.S. S.O.S. S.O.S.

I wish Marvin wasn't **so** good at singing. I also wish he wasn't currently making **SAND ANGELS** in the middle of my **S.O.S.** as part of his impromptu Justin Chase tribute performance.

'Get out of there. You're **RUINING** my sign!'

'I'm. So. Oh. Sorry!' Marvin sings sarcastically.

When he finally moves, I notice something **glistening** where he swept the sand away. Jutting out of the ground is the neck of a bottle.

55

I dig the bottle out of the sand and examine it. Inside is a rolled-up piece of tattered paper. A **real-life** message in a bottle! But before I have a chance to open it, Marvin snatches it out of my hand.

'I found that! Finders KEEPERS!' Marvin declares and **POPS** open the bottle. He slides out the roll of paper and unfurls it. I see his eyes **WIDEN** as they scan the page.

'Show me! What does it say?' I plead.

Marvin won't let me see. 'Allow me to read it to you.' He clears his throat dramatically, and then commences ...

Whoever finds this note, please send HELP! I am suffering and in constant pain. I fear for my sanity. I have been stuck on this unchartered island for what seems like an eternity with the lamest person on Earth ... Poo Boy!

Yours sincerely, Marvin King.

P.S. No autographs.

P.P.S. Floppy Doppy is the best.

Marvin smirks. I grab the paper out of his hand. That's not what the message says at all. It looks like a TREASURE MAP (well, half a treasure map, at least) of the island we're on now.

ACTUAL message in bottle

TREASURE ISLAND

MOUNT
SKULLMORE

CAVE OF
RICHES

BAY OF
BLOOD

JUNGLE
OF DOOM

GOLD
BEACH

'I think we're here.' I tap the map at GOLD BEACH.

'When we should be **HERE!**' Marvin points at the CAVE OF RICHES, then steals the map back. 'That's settled then. I'm off to find the treasure. I'm going to be famous **AND** rich! Are you coming, Crab Boy, or are you going to stay here and build sandcastles?'

The only way to reach that **X marks the spot** is via the BAY OF BLOOD or through the JUNGLE OF DOOM. **Neither** of those sound especially friendly.

'I think we should just wait here together to be safe.'

Marvin sighs. 'Urgh. You're such a boring baby. This place is **TINY.** I can see the cave from here! We'll have a nice bushwalk around the island, find the treasure in no time and be back for the rescue party.'

I glance over towards the jungle, which looks very jungle-y! I imagine what's **LURKING** in there, and shake my head.

'Fine. More treasure for ME. Later, loser!' Marvin collects his things and heads off down the beach in the direction of the trees.

And then it's just me. All **alone** in the middle of **NOWHERE** on a creepy deserted beach. All alone, except for the crabs.

And that seagull.

And **that** seagull.

And **THAT** seagull.

And **THOSE** seagulls.

The seagulls are rapidly multiplying!

All those beady, beady eyes **STARING** right at me are **triggering** some traumatic childhood seagull flashbacks.

And before they can turn me into a human hot chip, I'm running down the beach after Marvin, towards the **JUNGLE OF DOOM**, shouting **'WAIT FOR ME, WAIT FOR ME!'**

8:22am

We're only a few steps into the dense undergrowth and it is already abundantly clear that this was a **BAD IDEA**. And I **know** bad ideas!

I'm tagging along behind Marvin as we follow a **meandering** path deeper into the jungle. I don't want to get too close to him, but at the same time I don't want to be too far away from the only other person in a place named **'OF DOOM!'**.

The trees are getting taller now and blocking out the sun. The **deeper** we go, the DARKER it gets and the more I'm aware of the sounds surrounding us. There is an **awful** lot of

SLITHERING and RUSTLING

happening in the leaves as we **trudge** along. And my imagination is going into OVERDRIVE.

The tangled vines are looking more and more like **SNAKES**.

WHAT'S THERE

WHAT I'M SEEING

I'm blaming **WOLF GRUNTZ** for that. The scene from the *DUDE VS DEATH* snake special is on a repeat loop inside my head.

And then the mighty python will swallow their prey WHOLE!

I really, really don't want to be something's breakfast!

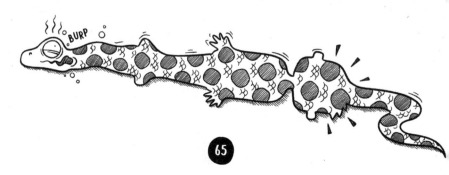

BURP

'Do you think there are snakes here?' I ask Marvin in a whisper, hoping for a reassuring 'Of course not'.

Instead he replies, **'DEFINITELY.** Snakes EVERYWHERE I bet, Poo Boy.'

I'm on extra-high alert for serpent spotting now. Each brush of leaves against my legs makes me **jump** as we continue our jungle trek.

8:35am

Did I mention the **BUGS?** There's creepy, crawly insects **CREEPING** and CRAWLING everywhere. On every tree. On every leaf. On every vine.

There's flying bugs too. Flitting and hovering and BUZZING around. So much **BUZZING.** And after yesterday's bee sting, I'm well and truly over insects.

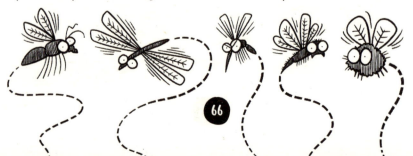

They don't seem to be over me, though. Or rather, they **ARE** all over me. Everywhere. Crawling, biting, stinging.

WOLF GRUNTZ

pops into my head again!

Why can I remember this but not my internet password?!

The mosquito is the deadliest creature in the world and can drink three times their own body weight in blood!

Insects are **SWARMING** me now. I'm doing my best to **shoo** and **SWAT** the bugs. It must look like another one of Dad's bad dance moves, as I hop from foot to foot while **slapping** different body parts – trying to get the insects before they get me!

'This is A-Grade content, Bug Boy!' Marvin laughs.

I look up from my creepy crawly **CONFLICT** and see Marvin fliming me again on his tablet. He gives me a thumbs up and a smarmy smile. But then he suddenly gets serious.

'**DON'T MOVE!** Whatever you do, don't move,' he warns me gravely. There's something in the tone of his voice that makes me freeze.

'Stay calm, but ... there's a **SNAKE** on your head!'

I gulp. I can **FEEL** it! **Wriggling** across the top of my hair. My brain is telling my body to stay still, but my body is saying:

'**GET IT OFF ME!**'

I blindly grab the snake and frantically **FLING** it to the ground, where it becomes quite clear that it was **NOT** actually a snake at all.

Marvin is laughing hysterically. 'Oops. My mistake. It was just a vine.'

I can feel the adrenalin pumping through my veins. My heart is **pounding,** my blood is boiling. I am **FUMING!**

I'm channeling my full-force **LASER EYES** straight at Marvin when I notice something lowering down onto his hair.

'There's a **SPIDER** on your head!' I tell him.

'Nice try, Vine Boy. You're so **PATHETIC!** Can't even come up with something original.'

And then I see the colour drain from Marvin's face as he feels the spider **scutter** down his forehead and stop on his nose.

'GET IT OFF ME!'

I watch on, quietly enjoying the poetic KARMA of the scene before me, as Marvin repeatedly **WHACKS** himself in the face with his tablet, trying unsuccessfully to **squish** the spider. I wonder if this footage is going to appear on the Marvelous Marvin channel? I would DEFINITELY like and subscribe to that!

9:16am

Are we lost?

10:03am

I think we're lost?

10:47am

Yep, we're lost.

11:13am

We've been walking for what feels like FOREVER through the Jungle of Doom. In circles? In spirals? In iscoceles triangles?

I don't know! At this point the map is **meaningless**, but Marvin is still certain we are on the right path to finding the fabled treasure.

'Just over this hill. Just around this bend. Just beyond these trees,' he keeps saying. His **positivity** is **IRRITATING**.

As is the fact that he looks like he's just stepped out of a fashion catalogue. Meanwhile I am covered in grime, **SLIME** and dirt. My clothes are **TORN**. My skin is covered in itchy, **bumpy** insect bites. How is this possible?

COMPARE THE PAIR

Sneakers STILL white! Not fair!

Plus, I am **EXHAUSTED.** My legs are **ACHING.**
I'm totally puffed. 'Too many video games!' is what Mum
would say. (But she does say that about everything.)

And just when I think the jungle couldn't get **worse** ...

RRRAAAAGGHHHHH!

A **terrifying**, high-pitched cry echoes through the treetops above us, sending a **GHOSTLY** chill down my spine. My knees are **knocking**. My teeth are CHATTERING.

The **SHRILL** voice calls out again, this time speaking.

'YOU SEARCH FOR GOLD
AND WEALTH UNTOLD,
BUT THOSE WHO DARE ...
BEWARE, BEWARE!'

Both Marvin and I **SCREAM** and start running, trying to get away from whoever, or **whatever**, is calling out to us.

Marvin is in the lead and each bendy branch he pushes out of his path **flings** back as he passes, slapping me in the face.

We keep sprinting, **spurred** on by the scary mystery voice, until we emerge at a small clearing, **SKIDDING** to an abrupt halt. We're seriously out of breath and **PERILOUSLY** out of path. Our toes are at a cliff's edge. In front of us is a **steep** drop down into a treacherous **RAVINE**.

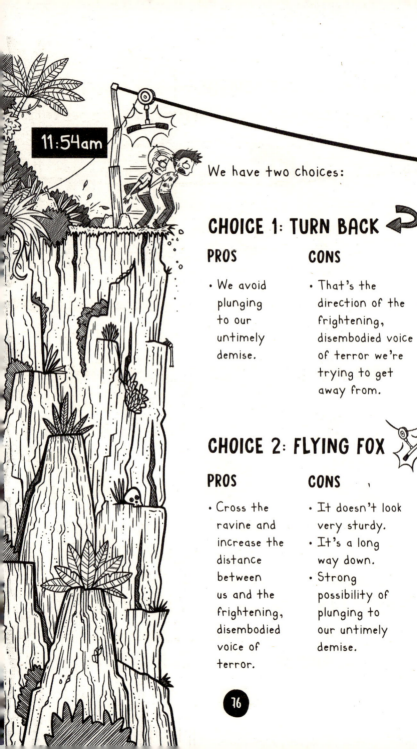

11:54am

We have two choices:

CHOICE 1: TURN BACK

PROS

- We avoid plunging to our untimely demise.

CONS

- That's the direction of the frightening, disembodied voice of terror we're trying to get away from.

CHOICE 2: FLYING FOX

PROS

- Cross the ravine and increase the distance between us and the frightening, disembodied voice of terror.

CONS

- It doesn't look very sturdy.
- It's a long way down.
- Strong possibility of plunging to our untimely demise.

NEITHER option is very appealing but the decision is quickly made for us when we hear the **screeching** cries of

'BEWARE, BEWARE!'

getting closer behind us.

'Let's go!'

We grab the flying fox and **LAUNCH** into the air. Gravity takes over and then we are **ZOOMING** along the zipline over the chasm.

There's a weird blinding

FLASH!

of light and then we reach the
other side. But we don't stop!

The cable continues into the undergrowth and so do we.

Our momentum **hurtles** us along and we explode through

trees,   bushes   and vines ...

WHACK

BOOF

ZONK

OUCH!   OUCH!   OUCH!

... until finally we land on the soft, springy floor of
the jungle. I **SPIT** out a mouthful of leaves and wipe
splattered bugs from my face.

I can't help but notice Marvin looks fine!

We survived the zipline, at least. And escaped the banshee!

`11:57am`

No, we didn't.

'BEWARE, BEWARE!'

the voice cries out again, getting **closer**. A **SHADOW** falls over us. We look up and see a **BLUR** of movement circling above. It **spirals** down, closer and **CLOSER**, until ...

... it lands right on Marvin's shoulder.

'BEWARE! BEWARE! WHO'S A PRETTY BOY, THEN?' The frightful **fury** pursuing us this whole time was actually just a talking PARROT – who seems to quite like Marvin.

The feeling is **mutual**. Marvin is smiling sweetly, gently stroking the parrot's head. He's repeating again and again in a baby-talk voice, 'You're a pretty boy! Yes, you are.'

I reach over to pat the bird's head too. And get rewarded with a beak bite on my finger!

YOUCH!

'I like this parrot A LOT!' Marvin beams. 'I think I'll call you SNAPPY!'

We're still trudging through the jungle. It's **WAY** past lunchtime and I haven't eaten since yesterday. I'm getting hungry. **Really** hungry. Even Snappy is starting to look a bit **TASTY!**

And after all that trekking and screaming and running and screaming I'm **THIRSTY** too. So **VERY** thirsty.

Marvin is feeling the same, announcing, 'I need something to eat. And something to drink.'

'**WHAT'S FOR DINNER?**' Snappy chimes in unhelpfully.

And then we reach a clearing in the jungle. A small **waterfall** is trickling into a SPARKLING pool surrounded by lush vegetation and beautiful flowers. It's a postcard perfect **OASIS**. In any other circumstances, the perfect place for a picnic.

'I'll find the water, you find the food,' Marvin decides, which seems WILDLY unfair. Even my nan could find the water without her glasses on. It's right **THERE!** But I'm too tired to fight.

'Fine! I'll find the food!' I grumble.

There **MUST** be something **edible** around here somewhere. Wolf Gruntz can survive anywhere on Mother Nature's plentiful bounty, but I know it's not that straightforward.

These berries are delicious AND nutritious…

…while these identical berries are toxic AND fatally poisonous.

I peer up into the trees. Maybe I'll spot something we can eat. I do spy some **COCONUTS** way up high. I'm **allergic** to certain nuts (that's why I have my allergy bracelet), but coconuts are fine for me.

NUT ALLERGY

I try **SHAKING** the spindly trunk of the tree, hoping some coconuts will fall down. The coconuts don't budge, but it looks like I've unwittingly woken a **MONKEY** who was resting high up in the leaves. And he's *not* happy!

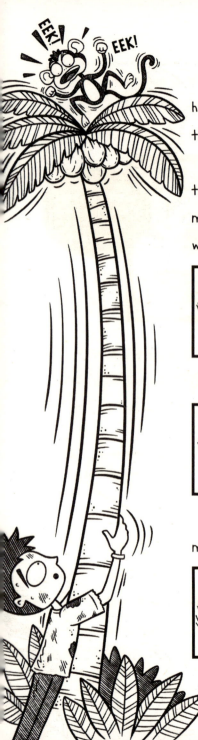

The monkey is **HOWLING**, hopping up and down like a toddler throwing a **TANTRUM**.

I **wave** at the monkey, trying to convey that I'm a friend. The monkey calms down and cheekily waves back.

I smile and the monkey smiles.

I poke out my tongue and the monkey pokes out his tongue.

I try my best to **MIME** throwing a coconut, hoping the monkey might throw one down for me. I won't be touring as a professional mime artist anytime soon, but I think I've done an OK job.

The monkey screeches and jostles around in the leaves and then **THROWS** something at me. It misses. And it's not a coconut either.

The projectile **splatters** on the ground next to me.

I wonder how the monkey found **MUD** up in a tree? And then the **smell** hits my nostrils and I realise **THAT'S NOT MUD** as the monkey takes aim again.

SCENE DELETED

BY THE CENSORS

(FOR YOUR OWN GOOD!)

Please enjoy these cute baby goat pictures instead ...

Apologies for the disruption to transmission.
We now resume our scheduled programming ...

12:47pm

I've washed off downstream. On the **negative** side, I **STILL** smell like monkey poo. On the **positive** side, all that treetop **TUMULT** did eventually knock down a fresh COCONUT!

Now I just have to **crack** it open.

IN MY HEAD

AHHHHH!
SO REFRESHING!

IN REALITY

AAARGGHH!
SO FRUSTRATING!

I'm getting **REALLY** annoyed! My mood is not improved when I notice Marvin casually reclining by the bank of the pool, filming me **FAIL** repeatedly.

'You could help!' I yell.

'Your job is the food, Coconut Boy. I found the drink.' He gestures with a flourish towards the water, where I spot a fish swimming.

Forget the coconut. We're having **SEAFOOD!**

GULP!

87

1:03pm

I roll up my pants and wade into the water, Wolf Gruntz style. I'm ready to **HUNT** some lunch with my bare hands and **lightning** reflexes!

LUNGE

DIVE

POUNCE

DANG!

DRATS!

PHOEY!

I try and try, but the fish is just too fast for me.

If only I had a **NET!** I wish Nan was here. She would crochet me a net! Then I remember – *I* can crochet, thanks to Nan's lessons.

I find some thin vines and use a crooked twig as a makeshift crochet hook and get **busy**, Nan in my head guiding the way.

I **made** a net! Not a great net. But it's a **NET!**

And it works. **Eventually.** After waiting ... waiting ... waiting ... waiting ... waiting ... waiting ... waiting ...

I **actually** catch a fish! Not a big fish. But it's a **FISH!**

SCOREBOARD
NAN VS GRUNTZ
1   0

SOB   SOB

DRINK THOSE TEARS, WOLFIE!

I'm holding it above my head like a trophy when a seagull **SWOOPS** down out of nowhere and **snatches** it! Adding fresh new content to my traumatic seagull experiences mental folder.

I'm so **FURIOUS**, I kick the coconut at my feet. And it splits **OPEN!**

Marvin and I both **pounce** on the coconut halves, clawing out the juicy flesh. It is so good to EAT again. **YUM!** But soon it's all gone.

'I'm still hungry,' Marvin moans.

'WHO'S A HUNGRY BOY, THEN?' Snappy squawks and takes flight into the tree tops. A moment later he returns, clutching a mango in his claws.

'EAT YOUR FRUIT!' he shrieks, sounding a bit like Mum (sorry, Mum, it's true), and drops the mango right on my head. I'm so happy to see more food, I don't even care.

THUNK

Marvin and I tear the mango open and DEVOUR the delicious pulp. While we're eating, Snappy is busy picking and dropping more fruit, like a feathered food delivery drone.

91

It's raining a tropical **FEAST** of fruity delights.

Guava Dragonfruit Lychees Starfruit Rambutan

And we **GORGE** ourselves!

2:28pm

Might have **OVERDONE** it on the fruit.

GROAN!

Not feeling so great in the tummy. There's that all too familiar feeling of **CHURNING** and **CRAMPS**. I can tell ... and **smell** ... that Marvin is suffering the same way.

As the silent farts intensify in **stench**, there is a silent understanding between us. We head off in separate directions for some privacy.

Time to quickly dig a hole before the **crisis** strikes!
I find a sheltered spot behind a tree and start
URGENTLY digging away with a stone. Making my own
toilet – Dad would be proud!

I'm scraping away the dirt, getting deeper, when I
strike something solid. I brush away the soil and reveal a
hard, shiny surface, almost glowing an irridescent blue.
Is this **BURIED TREASURE?** I dig around the object
and pluck it from the ground, holding the strange-looking,
jewelled **talisman** in my palm. It's **MESMERISING.**

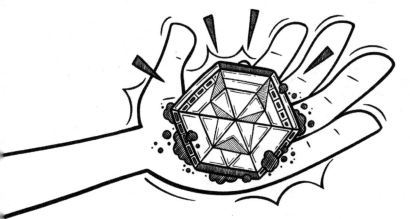

I want to get excited, but nature is calling. Quite loudly.
An **URGENT,** insistent grumbling that can't be ignored roars
from deep within my **GUTS.** I pocket the talisman, pull my
pants down, squat over my hole and brace for the **onslaught.**

SCENE DELETED

BY THE CENSORS

(WOAH! THAT WAS MESSY!)

Please enjoy these cute baby hedgehog pictures instead ...

Apologies for the disruption to transmission.
We now resume our scheduled programming ...

2:35pm

You would think I'd be used to this experience by now, but even I, a seasoned diarrhea professional, would rate that intestinal explosion as **INTENSE**. I may have also needed a **bigger** hole. But I think, at least, it is OVER.

And now I've got a **deja vu** loo situation. No toilet paper! Luckily there are lots of lush leaves around this time for my toilet paper substitute. My socks are safe!

PHEW! THAT'S A RELIEF!

The cool green of the leaves is almost **soothing**. And then it's **TINGLING**. And then it's **ITCHY** unbearably verging on **BURNING**. And then I belatedly remember another *DUDE VS DEATH* episode.

Beware of PLANTS!

This harmless looking leaf can cause rashes, swelling and even blisters upon contact with human skin.

RRRAAAAGGHHHHH!

I run, or rather **HOP**, with my pants around my ankles to the pool of water and **DUNK** my butt. The cool water gradually **EXTINGUISHES** my burning bottom.

Even though I don't want to hear it, I can still hear Marvin dealing with his own tummy **TROUBLES** in the distance, so I just sit and enjoy the chilled water. Snappy has flapped off somewhere so it's just me and my very own beautiful, outdoor bathtub in **paradise**. It's quite an **IDYLLIC** moment.

I make small circles with my hands, gently **gliding** my arms through the water, entranced by the reflected light dancing on the surface.

That's when I notice **something** on my hand.

NOM
NOM
NOM

I inspect it more closely, and recoil in horror. It's a **LEECH!** A blood-sucking, PARASITIC leech **gorging** on my skin.

'EEERRGGHHH!'

And there's one on my other hand too. And some on my wrists. And there's even more attached to my arms.

I stand bolt upright and nervously look **DOWN**.

I check front and back and my worst fears are **confirmed**. There are LEECHES **EVERYWHERE** down there. And by **everywhere** down there, I really mean ...

SCENE DELETED

BY THE CENSORS
(IT'S FOR THE BEST REALLY.)

Please enjoy these adorable little cow pictures instead ...

Apologies for the disruption to transmission.
We now resume our scheduled programming ...

SCENE DELETED

BY THE CENSORS

(OMG. THERE'S BLOOD!)

Please enjoy these sweet duckling pictures instead ...

Apologies for the disruption to transmission.
We now resume our scheduled programming ...

SCENE DELETED

BY THE CENSORS
(ALMOST DE-LEECHED NOW. HANG IN THERE!)

Please enjoy these heart-warming panda pictures instead ...

Apologies for the disruption to transmission.
We now resume our scheduled programming ...

3:13pm

'Wake up!'

I'm gently shaking Marvin, who chose the wrong moment to return to the pool. When he saw me removing the leeches from my nether regions, he **FAINTED**.

FLASHBACK

THUMP!

I'm pretty worried about him, but it looks like he's slowly regaining consciousness. His eyelids **flicker** open.

'Hello, Leech Boy,' Marvin murmurs.

I'm not so worried anymore!

3:20pm

Marvin has recovered and we're continuing on the treasure hunt. He's convinced we are closer than ever to the CAVE OF RICHES.

Snappy is perched on Marvin's shoulder, but occasionally flies up into the air and **FLUTTERS** around before returning to his post. The pair have formed quite the bond and I trail behind their little gang like a third wheel.

To make it **worse,** while I was trying my best to find us food at the oasis, Marvin used the time to train Snappy with some new phrases. So now I have to ENDURE the parrot randomly squawking out things like:

'BEWARE, BEWARE, POO BOY'S UNDERWEAR!' and 'WHO'S A TOILET BOY, THEN?'

Marvin thinks it is HILARIOUS!

I am over Marvin. I am over walking through the jungle. I am over **A LOT** of things right now.

LIST OF THINGS I AM OFFICIALLY OVER

 Marvin

 Seagulls

 Spiders

 Bugs

 Vines

 Walking

 Vines that look like snakes

 Sand in my undies

 Leaves

 Diarrhea

 Mud

 Jungle

 Talking parrots

 Thirst

 Monkeys

 Crabs

 Blood-sucking leeches

 Marvin

 Marvin

 Everything

Continues . . .

I'm mentally adding more to my **ever-growing** list when Snappy takes flight again. He flies ahead and circles back, squawking excitedly, **'AVAST YE, FOLLOW ME!!'**

Marvin and I pick up the pace and trail along behind the parrot as he leads us here:

I am shaking my head forcefully. 'There's **NO WAY** I'm going in there!'

'You heard Snappy. It's a shortcut to **GOLD!** Let's go!' Marvin is nodding firmly.

'I went into this jungle and I regret it! I am not going into a **BLACK HOLE** clearly signposted **DANGER!**'

'That's just an insurance thing or to deter treasure seekers, like us.'

It's a head-shaking/head-nodding stand off.

'I trust Snappy. Don't you?' Marvin asks.

I have a quick think about it. 'No. Not really!'

SNAPPY'S RAP SHEET

- Chased us across a ravine
- Tried to bite my finger off
- Dropped a mango on my head
- Calls me Poo Boy
- Actually likes Marvin

SNAPPER

'Well, we can't go back the way we came!' Marvin is **herding** me towards the tunnel entrance. 'I vote we go!' he says and gives me a little **PUSH.**

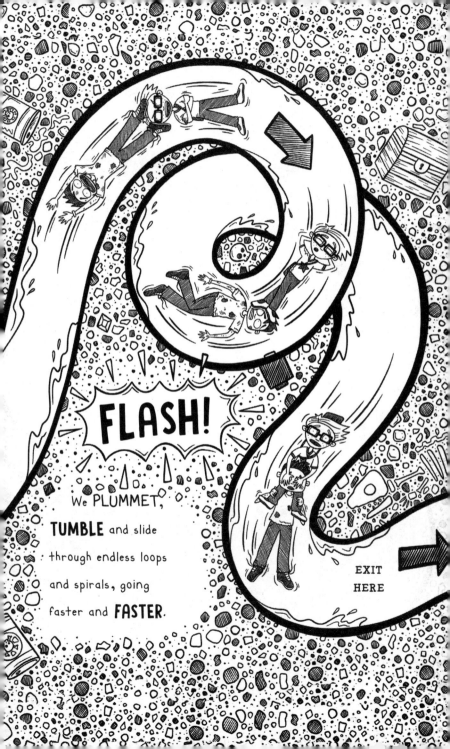

3:47pm

A small circle of light LOOMS up ahead, growing increasingly

larger as we **SPEED** through the slippery tunnel.

P.O.V.:
You're sliding
down a
bizarre tunnel
towards a
circle of light

And it looks like, just maybe, the shortcut WORKED!

Have we actually found the treasure?

Are we now filthy **RICH?!**

We EXPLODE into the open air, **JETTISONED** out of the tunnel in a **deluge** of water and a tangle of limbs.

Soggy and SHAKEN, we stand, ready to survey our pirates' **BOUNTY** and claim our new-found **wealth.**

But there are **no** treasure chests. **NO** towering piles of gold and jewels. Just this **SIGN** pointing towards a **very** familiar-looking place.

GOLD BEACH

For a deserted island there's a remarkable amount of signage!

We walk silently, in **DENIAL**, along the shoreline of the sandy peninsula. Thers's an abandoned life raft, an airplane seat and a rocky sign spelling ...

We are right back where we started!

My anguished cry ECHOES out across the empty beach.

Marvin hasn't handled the setback well either. He is **pacing** up and down the sand, studying the treasure map, trying to work out what went wrong. He looks possessed as he mutters and **MUMBLES** under his breath.

'So close. So close. So close.'

His eyes are **DARTING** from the map clutched in his hand up to the island. He grabs my shirt and exclaims in **EXASPERATION**, 'We were so close. So close. It's right **THERE!**' He points over the bay dramatically.

I look over to the CAVE OF RICHES across the water. Marvin's right. It really isn't far. I could **easily** swim that distance. It's probably only a dozen Olympic pools across.

No sweat for a Swim Star!

The fact it is labelled **BAY OF BLOOD** on the map, though, is **slightly** off-putting. The **JUNGLE OF DOOM** certainly lived up to its name!

But that might also mean the **CAVE OF RICHES** is **ACTUALLY** filled with treasure! I still have that jewelled **talisman** I found safely stashed in my pocket (I haven't told Marvin – so he doesn't try to steal it), so I know there really **IS** treasure on the island.

What if there is an **ENTIRE** cave filled with more of the same? I have to admit the thought makes me **excited.**

For that brief moment in the tunnel, when I believed we had found **GOLD**, I was overjoyed and happily spending all that money in my head ...

MY UNLIMITED WEALTH MENTAL SHOPPING LIST

A fancy gold-plated toilet for Dad

Happy tears

A gold-plated teapot and gold-plated antique mirror for Nan

To replace the one I broke

A gold-class ticket to anywhere in the world – or even space – for Mum

She can do the countdown!

A gold-plated state-of-the-art drawing tablet for Mia

An upgrade on her notepad

And I would be the most **POPULAR** guy at school. No-one would even remember the pool incident.

I could pay to have all traces of **POO BOY** removed from the internet. No more videos. No more **memes!**

Now that I think about it, I'm suddenly **VERY** keen to find that treasure.

'The water's calm. It's not really that far. We could take the raft,' I suggest to Marvin. His eyes **LIGHT UP** like mine.

KA-CHING!

KA-CHING!

'Let's do it!'

Goodbye, POO BOY. Hello, **GOLDEN BOY!** Obscene wealth, we're on our way!

4:10pm

We drag the raft across the sand to the bayside of the beach and launch into the tranquil waters of the BAY OF BLOOD.

Marvin has appointed himself navigator, even though it's pretty obvious where we're heading. He's perched at the bow of the raft, life jacket on, map in hand, acting like he's **the Captain**. Meanwhile, I'm stuck on rowing duty with my dodgy DIY paddle.

It's way harder than it looks, and I'm working up a sweat. My legs were aching during the jungle trek. Now it's my arms that are protesting. I can hear Mum in my head saying, 'Too many video games!'

When I'm stinking rich, i.e. **VERY SOON,** I vow I will only travel via engine-powered vehicles. Right now, though, I'm just **STINKING.**

I look back over my shoulder to gauge how much progress we've made. Hardly any! But I do notice we're being trailed by a **FIN,** slicing through the water like a knife.

'The dolphins are back!' I cheer to Marvin. 'Maybe they can push us!' I add hopefully. 'Come here, Flipper!' I pat the water to get its attention.

The fin glides towards us and starts circling the raft. I'm **NOT** getting happy, playful dolphin **VIBES** from the fin.

Instead, I'm getting man-eating ...

'SHARK!'

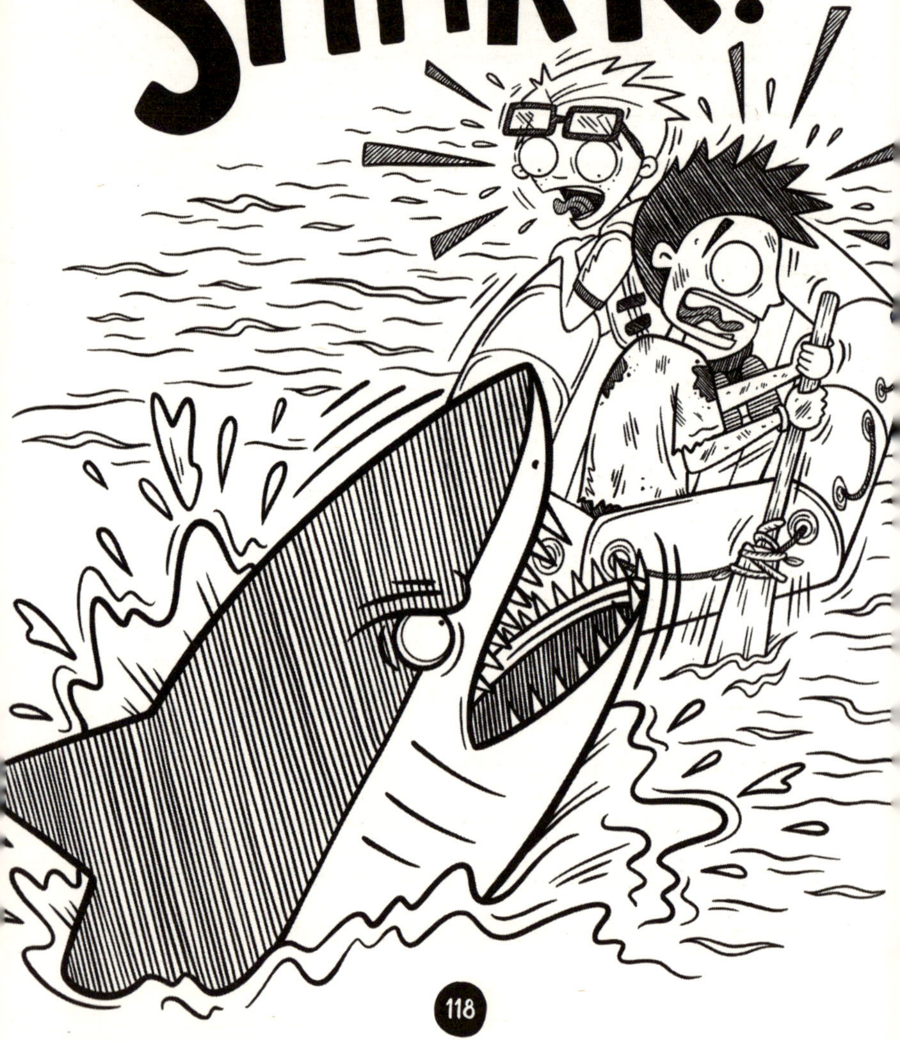

They say humans evolved the fight-or-flight response as a SURVIVAL mechanism.

And while I like to think of myself more as a FLIGHT kind of guy, for some reason right now I have chosen FIGHT! I suddenly go full PIÑATA mode on the shark, channeling my inner six-year-old pumped up on lollies and cake at a party.

I'm landing some **impressive** blows and it looks like I'm inflicting some serious damage on the shark's skin, which slowly peels away to reveal a ...

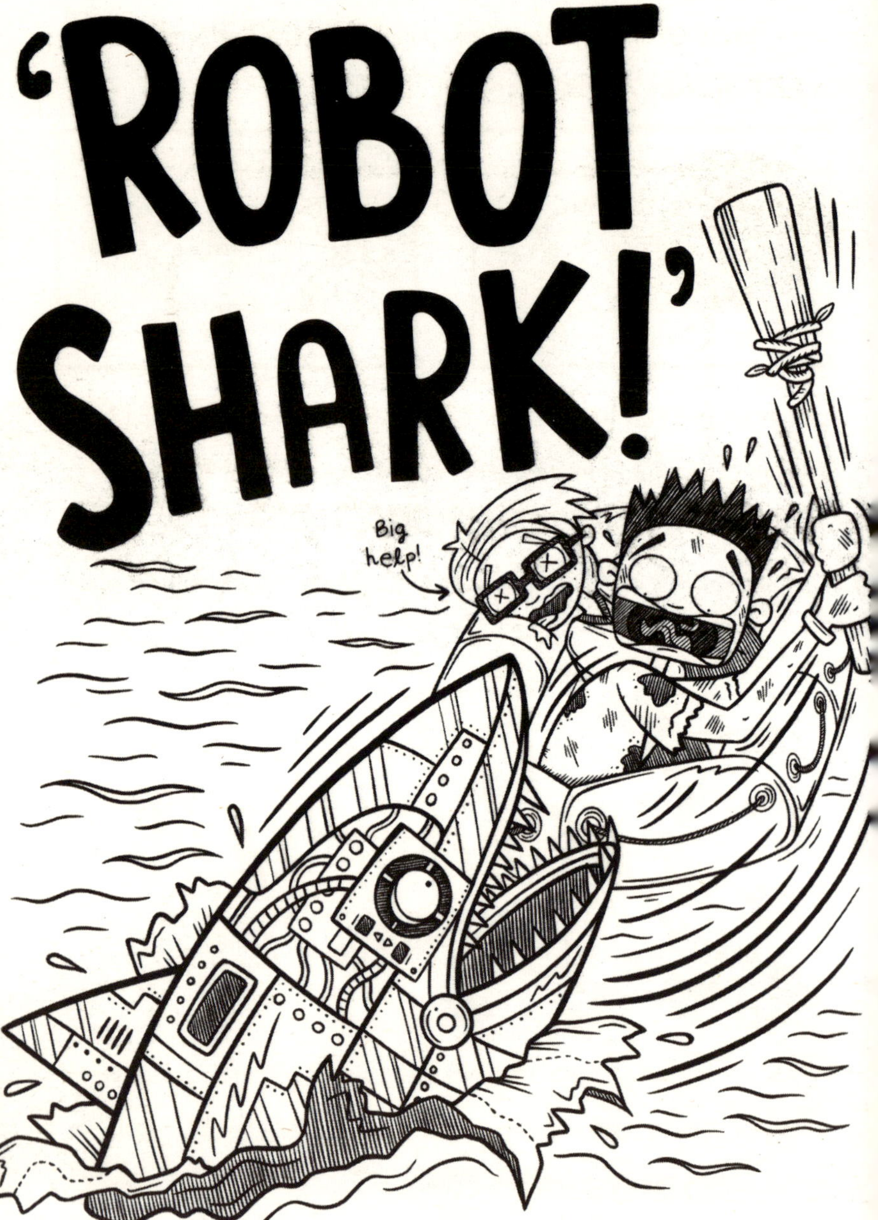
'ROBOT SHARK!'
Big help!

Wolf Gruntz has not covered **ROBOT SHARKS** in ANY episode of *DUDE VS DEATH.*

Thanks for nothing, Wolf!

I have a **random** thought that I need to tell Mia about the robot shark. I bet she could do something **AMAZING** with the idea for her awesome unicorn video game. If I survive long enough to tell her! **FOCUS!**

In any other scenario, a robot shark would be **extremely** cool. Just not this particular scenario where I'm about to be **EATEN** alive by one. Its mechanical **JAWS** are opening and closing theatrically as it gets closer.

As I continue hitting it with my paddle, the robot shark appears to be **MALFUNCTIONING**. Smoke and sparks are **pouring** out from its battered circuitry.

CLANG!

I'm COWERING, bracing to be **devoured** in a single **BITE**, as the shark advances. I stare fearfully into its glowing, beady red **EYE**, and, as it advances, I can see it is labelled.

CLOSE UP

ON
△
▽
OFF

In a final act of desperation, I spin the paddle and use the pointy end to **POKE** the robot shark's eye.

The red glowing eyeball **fades** to black and the robot shark seems to be powering down. The sparks **FIZZLE** out. It stops pursuing us. And, in slow motion, its gaping wide **JAWS** are slowly closing.

We're **NOT** safe. The razor sharp teeth of the robot shark **pierce** the fabric of the inflatable raft.

As air GUSHES out of the punctured raft, we're propelled into the air like we're riding an out-of-control **MAGIC CARPET** into a whole new world of terror.

We zip and zoom **HAPHAZARDLY** across the bay with as much finesse as a loose, untied balloon **ricocheting** around a room.

ZIIIIIIP!

As the last gasps of air **splutter** from the deflated raft, we miraculously land with a **THUD** at the yawning mouth of the **CAVE OF RICHES!**

ZOOOOOM!

THUD!

Inside it looks like a big-budget **BLOCKBUSTER** pirate movie set. An abandoned sailing ship with tattered sails has run aground in the **grotto**. Gold and jewels spill from the ruptured hull into the shallow water. Further back in the cave, there are mountains of treasure chests and coins **SPARKLING** like stars in the night sky.

As we take a step inside, the cave seems to automatically come to **life**.

Even though there is no breeze in the cavern, the **JOLLY ROGER** flag on the ship's mast starts **FLUTTERING**.

An **eerie** mist rolls out in tendrils across the water.

 **CREAKING** and **RATTLING**

sounds come from inside the ship.

And I notice that the eyes of all the **SKULLS** littered amongst the treasure begin to GLOW.

We pause in our tracks. The spookiness is undeniable, but the jackpot of riches right in front of us is also undeniable.

Part of me is saying, 'Run, NOW, you nincompoop!'

The other part is saying '**KA-CHING!**' much LOUDER.

'Let's get some treasure FAST, and get out of here even **FASTER**,' I suggest as the plan of action.

Marvin is already ahead of me. He's raced over to the biggest pile of treasure and is making angels in the GOLD.

It is MESMERISING being surrounded by so much sparkle. I actually start to **FROLLICK** in the treasure too!

We're snapped out of our treasure party by a loud ghostly **MOAN** that reverberates throughout the cave. The mist has spread and we are now shrouded in a thick fog. It's getting decidedly CREEPY.

'We need to get out of here!' I **whimper**.

'Not without the treasure,' Marvin insists. 'Let's load up this empty minecart. Get the good stuff, then we go.'

I hesitantly agree and launch into high-speed video game loot-collecting mode.

TREASURE HUNTERS

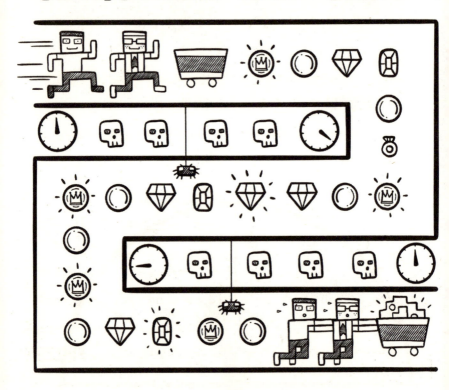

The mine cart is now **OVERFLOWING.**

BEFORE AFTER

I don't know how much it's worth (I don't have much experience with piles of gold), but I'm thinking this must make us at least ~~millionaires~~ ... ~~billionaires~~ ... ~~trillionaires~~ ... GAZILLIONAIRES!

I'm going to have to replace my piggy bank with a vault!

First, we have to wheel this thing out of here. Which is easier said than done. The cart is on tracks and too **HEAVY** to lift. We're **struggling** to push it off the rails in the direction of the exit when we're suddenly **FROZEN** in place.

'YO HO HO!'

A sinister **BOOMING** laugh echoes throughout the cave, hanging in the air and filling me with **DREAD**.

We spin around in **TERROR** and see a figure is slowly rising into view on the ship from below deck.

Even in my current state of intense **FEAR**, I have to admit it's an impressive and **dramatic** entrance! The PIRATE CAPTAIN holds his pose like a statue, brandishing a cutlass in the air.

As if on cue, Snappy flies in from outside and perches on the pirate's shoulder screeching:

'BEWARE, BEWARE!'

I *KNEW* that parrot couldn't be trusted!

The pirate shakes his sword **menacingly** and his deep, scratchy voice BLASTS out like surround sound.

'SCURVY DOGS! WHO DARES TO ENTER ME CAVE OF RICHES? ARRRRRRRRRRRRRRRR!'

Marvin is **vigorously** pointing at me. '**HE** dared. All **HIS** idea. I said not to!'

The pirate pays absolutely no heed.

'**UNLEASH THE CURSE OF BARNACLE BONES! ARRRRRRRRRRRRRRR!**' he shouts gravely.

There is a loud **CLAP** of thunder and streaks of **lightning INSIDE** the cave! The **CREAKING** and **RATTLING** from within the ship intensifies and a ghostly crew of pirate apparitions pours out towards us.

Presiding over the spirits, the captain is repeating **'ARRRRRRRRRRRRRRR!'** again and again, like he's stuck on a loop. His eye is glowing red and then ...

... his head starts **SPINNING** and **FLIES** off his neck!

We're losing our heads too. Just figuratively for now. We're **SCREAMING** in terror as we back away from the advancing pirate ghosts.

We **trip** over our own feet and fall backwards into the minecart. It starts rolling into the mineshaft, going faster and **FASTER**, with the ghosts in **PURSUIT**.

AAAARRRGGGHHHH!

AAAARRRGGGHHHH!

It seems we've outrun the ghosts, but now we're accelerating straight into this ...

DEAD END!

Literally!

I predict this is going to hurt. **A LOT!**

AAAARRRGGGHHHH!

We brace for the **IMPACT** as we **plough** right into the ...

SOUVENIR SHOP ?!
THANKS, TREASURE SEEKERS
HOPE YOU ENJOYED THE RIDE
PLEASE EXIT THE VEHICLE
BRING ALL YOUR BELONGINGS
HATS
CANDLES

MESSAGE IN A BOTTLE

SNOWDOMES

MONEY BOX

T-SHIRTS

I ♥

YO HO HO

X
MARKS
THE SPOT

SOFT TOYS

FRIDGE MAGNETS

TEASPOONS

Something for Nan!

PIRATE UNDIES
2 FOR 1 SALE

Marvin and I climb out of the minecart and **stumble** into a deserted gift shop. Shell shocked, **STUNNED** and very tempted by the clean underwear on sale.

We're trying to piece together what's happened.

141

There's a whole wall of digital screens.

My eyes are CLOSED in every photo

WICKED WILD WATERSLIDE

MINECART MAYHEM GHOST TRAIN

I swear I was just scratching my nostril!

Another wall is taken up by a giant (half) familiar map.

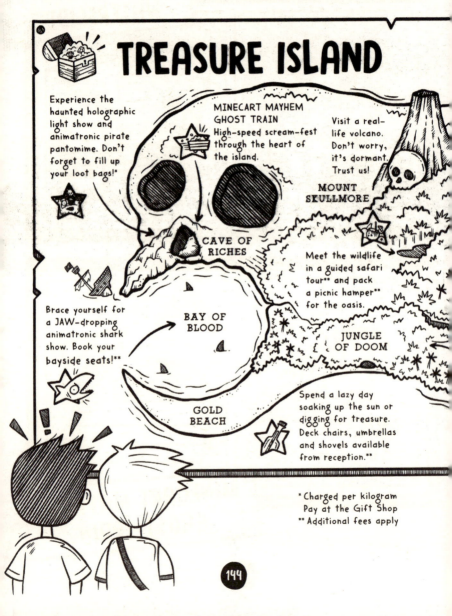

TREASURE ISLAND

Experience the haunted holographic light show and animatronic pirate pantomime. Don't forget to fill up your loot bags!*

MINECART MAYHEM GHOST TRAIN
High-speed scream-fest through the heart of the island.

Visit a real-life volcano. Don't worry, it's dormant. Trust us!

MOUNT SKULLMORE

CAVE OF RICHES

Meet the wildlife in a guided safari tour** and pack a picnic hamper** for the oasis.

Brace yourself for a JAW-dropping animatronic shark show. Book your bayside seats!**

BAY OF BLOOD

JUNGLE OF DOOM

GOLD BEACH

Spend a lazy day soaking up the sun or digging for treasure. Deck chairs, umbrellas and shovels available from reception.**

* Charged per kilogram
  Pay at the Gift Shop
** Additional fees apply

ADVENTURE FUNPARK™

BE A PIRATE FOR A DAY!

AHOY THERE, MATEYS! WELCOME TO THE WORLD'S FIRST FULLY-IMMERSIVE PIRATE-THEMED HOLIDAY RESORT!

CAFETERIA
All-you-can-eat fine dining.***

HOTEL
Poolside luxury accommodation.

GIFT SHOP
Bring home some "treasured" memories. (See what we did there!)

PADDLEBOAT PANDEMONIUM
Hours of water fun in our novelty vessels.*****

WICKED WILD WATER SLIDE
The perfect slip and slide shortcut to the beach

Keep an eye out for our real life mascots **POLLY THE TALKING PARROT** and **MARVIN THE CHEEKY MONKEY.**

FANTASTIC FLYING FOX
Race across the ravine in this thrilling activity.**** Don't look down!

Ha, ha, Marvin!

*** 'Fine' in this context is defined as 'acceptable' not 'superior'
**** Insurance recommended (**)
***** Charged per minute

™ Steel Corp.

BARNACLE BONES

145

This **ENTIRE** time we've been 'stranded' in a **THEME PARK?!** But where are all the staff? The other tourists? It's like a **GHOST TOWN.** I wander around, **dazed,** in disbelief.

Marvin has returned to our minecart and is inspecting our treasure. He suspiciously holds a gold coin between his fingers and then **SNAPS** it in half, like it's one of Nan's biscuits.

GOOD

BAD

He starts sobbing. 'It's fake. This whole place is **FAKE!**' He's **BLUBBERING** uncontrollably.

And I find myself giving him a comforting **hug.** 'It's OK. We're alive and it's civilisation at least. We can finally call for help!'

WAH WAH!

Marvin tries his tablet, but it's out of battery charge. There **must** be a phone or computer here somewhere in the building. We start exploring.

This Souvenir Shop leads into a cafeteria. There are no people, but there is **FOOD!** This is a *real* CAVE OF RICHES.

We run straight for the DESSERT BAR and start stuffing our faces, like pigs at a trough!

Marvin spots the **DRINKS** fridge and grabs some bottles. He hands one to me, taking me off guard. Last time he did that it was an EXPLODING booby-trapped rocket bottle. This time it's just a regular soft drink, like he's sharing a drink with a friend.

We '**CHEERS**' our fizzy drinks before gulping them down.

Definitely overdid the ALL-YOU-CAN-EAT dessert bar and fizzy drinks! I need a rest room stop.

I find the adjacent bathrooms and I almost shed a tear of joy when I see a proper porcelain **TOILET**. After that unholy hole experience in the jungle, I'm finally beginning to understand Dad's **obsession** with these modern marvels! We'll have to make a visit to the Toilet Appreciation Museum together once I'm back home.

There's toilet paper too. Triple ply! Forget gold and jewels. This is genuine **TREASURE!**

Which gives me a new idea for Dad's business. I can't wait to tell him all about it.

THE PIRATE PLUMBER!

YE OLDE POOP DECK

THARS ME SON

We've found a CONTROL ROOM. There's a wall of monitors, computers and phones. And lots and lots of buttons.

Unfortunately, there's still no reception when we try to call for help. We can't log onto their internet or connect to any wifi. It's so **FRUSTRATING!**

As I tap away at the keyboards and press **random** buttons, I manage to turn on the monitors. They're showing security **SURVEILLANCE** footage from around the island.

We can see ourselves in the control room.

I **rewind** back and see us in the cafeteria from a few moments ago.

I go further back and see me and the **LEECH** incident from a few hours ago.

Marvin has **FAINTED** again at the sight, so while he is passed out in the chair I decide to rewind back even further and work out **exactly** what happened on the island.

I've cracked the case like one of those **OBSESSIVE** true crime detectives. As Marvin wakes up I explain my discoveries.

Late yesterday, a severe tropical storm **EMERGENCY WARNING** was issued and **EVERYONE** on the island was ordered to **evacuate** immediately.

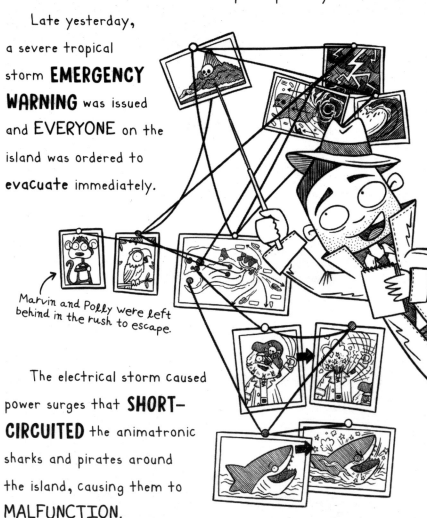

Marvin and Polly were left behind in the rush to escape.

The electrical storm caused power surges that **SHORT-CIRCUITED** the animatronic sharks and pirates around the island, causing them to **MALFUNCTION**.

'And **THAT'S** why we're all **ALONE** on this island being attacked by robot **sharks** and headless **pirates**!'

As I wrap up my explanation, I'm waiting for some appreciative applause from Marvin, but instead the whole room begins to **TREMBLE**. It feels like we're inside one of those snowdomes from the Gift Shop being **SHAKEN** around!

Why do they have snowdomes for a tropical island?!

WISH I WASN'T HERE

WISH YOU WERE HERE

The shaking subsides. There is a second of complete stillness and silence, and then emergency sirens start **FLASHING** and blaring an ear-piercing **WAIL**.

'CODE RED!

EVACUATE ISLAND!'

'Maybe it's just a drill,' I say hopefully.

'THIS IS NOT A DRILL. EVACUATE ISLAND!'

I notice a sign on the wall.

ISLAND CODES

▨	YELLOW	...........................Pee in the pool
▨	BROWN	......................Poo in the pool
▨	GREEN WITH ORANGE CHUNKS	......Spew in the pool
▨	RED	...............................Volcano erupting

SERIOUSLY? Now we're dealing with a **VOLCANO?!**

Just to recap:

☑ I accidentally ejected mid-air from a plane.

☑ I got stuck in an inflatable raft in the middle of nowhere with the absolute **WORST** person in the world.

☑ I was intimidated by seagulls, nipped by crabs, bitten by bugs, assaulted by imaginary snakes, lacerated by leeches, hunted by robotic sharks and hounded by holographic ghosts.

☑ **PLUS,** I was victimised by a poo-slinging monkey and a mango-dropping, trash-talking parrot.

☑ And now this whole, cursed fake island is rattling because a **VOLCANO** that is supposed to be dormant is about to **ERUPT!**

MY UNHAPPY PLACE

I NEED A HOLIDAY!

The control room begins to **SHAKE** again and the wall of monitors **flickers** on and off.

It's becoming
DISTRESSINGLY clear
that we need to ...

We're screaming (AGAIN!) and bolting as fast as we can away from the rumbling volcano. It is belching clouds of SMOKE and spitting chunks of LAVA. We need to get off this island fast. Our only chance is the jetty.

We're hoping for this:

Instead we get this:

High-speed jet boat

Rubber ducky paddleboat

We have no other option. We jump on the DUCKY and start PEDALLING out into the safety of the ocean.

No matter how fast we PUMP our legs, the pedal-powered rubber ducky just **putters** along at a snail's pace.

'POLLY WANTS A QUACKER!'

I'm am PUFFED. I feel like Dad on his stationary exercise bike during one of his health kicks. There's a lot of sweating and huffing happening while getting absolutely nowhere!

WHEEZ

WHEEZ

I glance back towards the island, hoping to see we've put some **substantial** distance between us and the volcano. We haven't. And there's a FIN trailing us **AGAIN!**

158

Another robot shark to deal with! At least now I know the ON/OFF button trick. But I have to think fast as the shark is approaching, jaws wide open.

I grab the umbrella and close it to make a **SPEAR**. I take aim for the **beady** eye and then poke the ON/OFF button as hard as I can.

SQUELCH

But the shark **doesn't** power down. It **FLARES** up! And I quickly realise that this is not, in fact, a malfunctioning, out-of-control animatronic shark. It's a ...

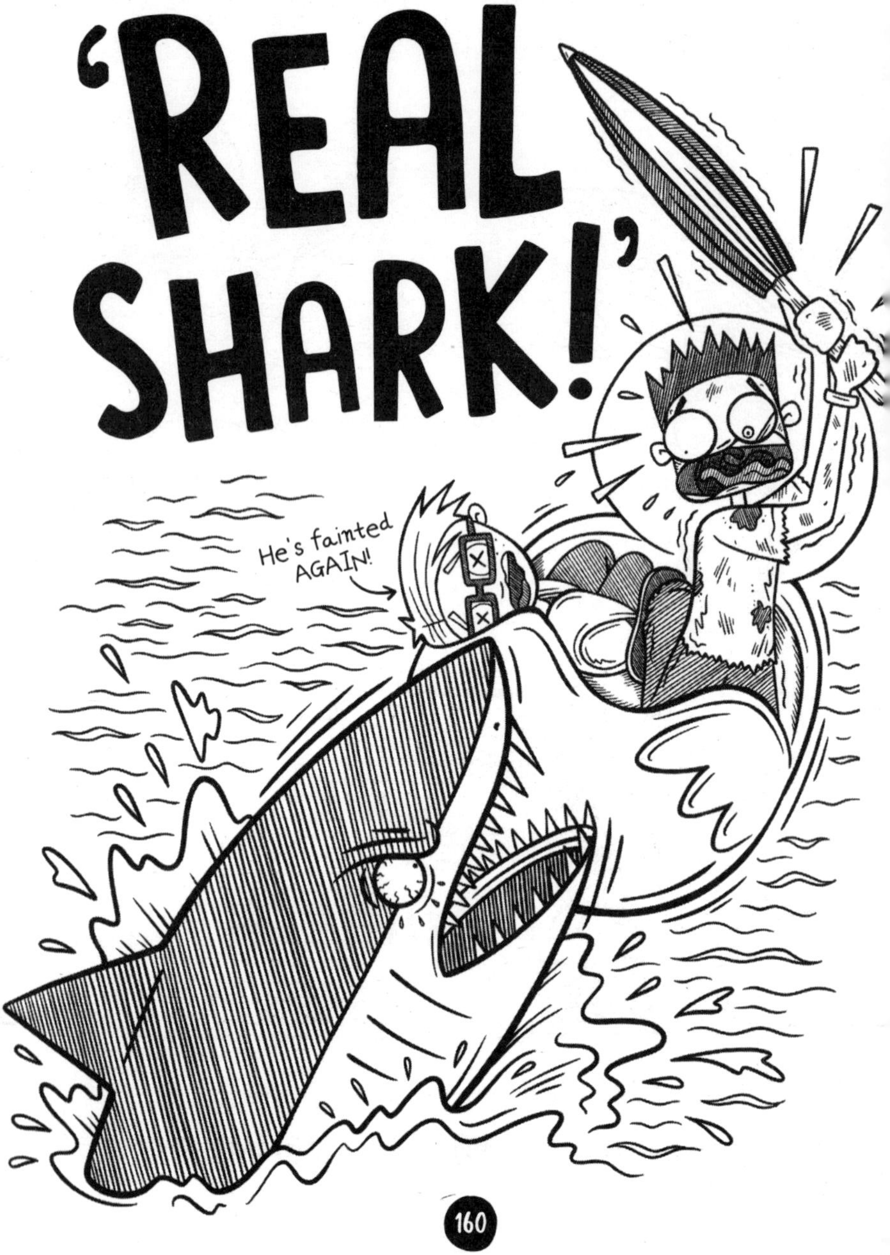
'REAL SHARK!'
He's fainted AGAIN!

And the real shark is now **VERY** angry. It DEVOURS the umbrella in one **bite**.

I'm left holding basically a TOOTHPICK, which the shark will probably use to clean its rows of **RAZOR-SHARP** teeth once it turns us into human **chicken nuggets**.

This is it. There's no more escaping. The shark moves in for its final attack. **I WANT MY MUMMY!**

And, out of nowhere, there she is.

MUM!

On a jet ski!

Speeding straight towards us!

SCREAMING,

'YOU'RE IN SO MUCH TROUBLE!'

But she's **not** yelling at me. She's yelling at the SHARK!

Forget ...

You're about to witness ...

The hunter has become the **hunted!** Mum launches herself straight at the shark and unleashes an unrelenting BARRAGE of her **LETHAL** martial arts moves.

The shark **never** stood a chance. It RETREATS to the depths of the ocean, realising two human chicken nuggets aren't worth the **BEATING**.

Mum pulls up alongside the paddleboat and sweeps me into her arms for one of her patented breath-blocking **EMBRACES**. After the extended hug, she **smothers** me in kisses.

And then Mum's eyebrows change **DIRECTION**.

FROM THIS

TO THIS

Here we go.

'Oh, you've got some explaining to do, **Justin Chase**. You are in SO MUCH **TROUBLE!**'

As Mum takes a breath in the middle of her TIRADE, I use the pause to ask the question that's been plaguing me since she turned up on the jet ski to save the day ...

'How did you find me?!' I ask **bewildered.**

Mum hesitates before answering, 'A mother always knows.'

'No! Really! How did you actually pin point my location?!'

Mum sighs. 'OK. The truth is there's a GPS TRACKING DEVICE in your allergy bracelet. I can track you on my phone at all times. Just to make sure you're not breaking any rules. It's perfectly legal and for your own good. Don't give me that look. You're the one who's in TROUBLE!'

This explains SO MUCH in my life!

PREVIOUSLY MYSTERIOUS MUM SIXTH-SENSE MOMENTS

You didn't walk directly home from school!

You didn't cross at the pedestrian crossing!

You went to the fast food place!

'And **LUCKY** for you I *do* track you!' Mum recovers. 'We only just got back online after the storm yesterday and I find out you're **MISSING!** (P.S. Your dad is in SO MUCH TROUBLE for agreeing to that unaccompanied plane ride and ridiculous TV show!) I checked my app right away and there you were running around on the next island across. I notified the authorities, but I was **CLOSER,** so I jumped straight on a jet ski.'

And now it's time for another Mum **HUG.**

6:10pm

The **reinforcements** have finally arrived! On the horizon, I can see and hear ships and helicopters approaching. A mixture of official **RESCUE** vessels and authorities, as well as a few **TV NEWS** choppers.

We're **signalling** with our arms to get their attention and they head towards us. Just in time too, as the volcano on the island is really starting to **ERUPT** now.

All the COMMOTION has roused Marvin. He looks up and sees the circling helicopters. And he notices the CAMERAS. He's never been happier in his life.

'I'M SAVED!'

The helicopter hovering above throws out a ladder that I somehow manage to **catch**.

Marvin **snatches** the rung out of my hand and starts climbing up first. I'm right behind him, eager to get to saftey. Marvin is taking his time, though, posing for the cameras filming our rescue.

He's waving grandly when he SLIPS ...

... and
PLUMMETS,
grabbing my
jeans ...

... which start
sliding down my
legs, lower and
LOWER ...

... until a hand
grasps my arm
and pulls us up.

It's **VLAD!** My new stepdad. So skinny, but apparently very strong. (Not surprising as super-strength is a well-known **VAMPIRE** power.)

'You ruined my honeymoon,' he states matter-of-factly in his **monotone** voice staring directly into my soul with his icy eyes. It's a relief when Mum clambers up the ladder into the helicopter behind Marvin.

'Let's get out of here!' she exclaims, and the chopper veers off, leaving the erupting volcano and harrowing island **ORDEAL** behind us.

6:23pm

Mum goes into full nurse-mode, checking Marvin and I over with the first-aid kit while trying to ignore the multiple lawyers from **WAKE UP!** inside the helicopter with us.

Thanks to the air-tight contract Dad and Ms King signed, despite our island detour we are still locked in to our appearance on the show, which has been postponed to tomorrow. Until then, we are all their 'VIP guests'.

We land on a private helipad in MEGA CITY and step out of the helicopter to a **ROCKSTAR** welcome.

  We're surrounded by **paparazzi** and fans shouting our names. Well, they're technically shouting **'Marvin'** and **'Poo Boy',** but it seems like we REALLY are **FAMOUS!**

  Marvin is lapping up the attention, **basking** in the glow of the camera flashes. He's waving and even blowing kisses.

We're all ushered into a **limousine,** where two people are already waiting inside.

'Good evening, our sensational SUPERSTARS! We're the producers of *Wake ...*'

'OH, YOU ARE IN SO MUCH TROUBLE!' Mum launches into an impressive DIATRIBE aimed directly at the unsuspecting producers.

As the limo rolls out, and Mum shares her thoughts, I check out the mini TV screen by my seat. It's playing the promotional video advertising us on *WAKE UP!* tomorrow.

I flick through the other channels and I start to get the impression that our disappearance was a pretty BIG deal.

We pull up outside a **FANCY** hotel. The producers appear to have **aged** twenty years in twenty minutes.

BEFORE MUM

AFTER MUM

My dad and Marvin's mum are waiting in the foyer for us. They **RUSH** out to greet us and it's bear **HUGS** all round.

'**HEART-WARMING!** Now do that again so we can film it from another angle,' one of the producers directs us.

Mum meets Dad's brand new fiancee for the first time as our parents all **politely** say hello to each other, **VERY** aware that there is a film crew present.

7:55pm

We're taken by elevator to the **VVVIP** (Very, Very, Very Important Person) floor. It is **PALATIAL!** We each get our very own lavish personal suite.

My suite is in-between Mum's room and Dad's room so they can both check on me via adjoining doors, but essentially I have this incredible pad all to myself. **SWEET** indeed!

There are two giant **GIFT BASKETS** waiting for me.

NO, THANKS!   ## YES, PLEASE!

Tropical Fruit

Not again!

Deluxe Chocolates!

Expensive!

Brand New Phone!

Perfect coz my old one went flying!

Manic Mayhem Battle Battalion Shoot Squad IX!

It's not even released yet!!

There's also a luxurious bathrobe and pair of super-fluffy slippers that fit perfectly. And a **GIANT**, sumptuous king-size bed as bouncy as a trampoline! We're allowed to order **anything** on the menu for dinner from room service.

I'm in **HEAVEN**.

8:11pm

'EEEEEKKKKKKKKKK!'

There's a high-pitched **SCREAM** from Dad's room.

I rush in through the adjoining door to find him hugging the toilet in his ritzy ensuite.

He's not throwing up, though. He is actually **hugging** the toilet. It's one of those hi-tech-gadget type toilets with a seat warmer and massage functions. He looks up at me with tears in his eyes.

'I've dreamt of this day my whole life, Juz Chuz!'

Dad's in **HEAVEN** too!

8:15pm

I decide to test out my new phone by video-calling Nan.

She's not great with technology, so most of the call is me looking up her **NOSE**.

You had us all worried, young man!

177

Nickers says hello too.

And so does Mia, who had popped over to check on me.

I'm so glad you're OK!

I tell her **ALL** about my Wednesday.

8:45pm

A kiss goodnight on the forehead from both Mum and Dad before they head off to their rooms.

MWAH! MWAH!

8:50pm

I get a message from Mia. She's sent a **ROBOT SHARK UNICORN** sketch for me.

And I was right. It *is* **AMAZING!**

Thanks for the inspo!

8:55pm

While I'm on my phone, I reluctantly decide to check the figures on the Poo Boy video. Over **2 BILLION** views now!

And then I see Marvin has already started uploading **NEW** videos from the island today. I can't believe that guy is going to become my **step-brother**!

9:30pm

I promised Mum I would go to sleep now. I have to be up extra early tomorrow.

I **AM** tired, but I can't go to sleep. Not when there's the brand new, not-even-officially-released **MMBBSS IX** video game, a console and a giant screen in the same room!

I **sneak** out of bed, get set up on the sofa and start the game, fighting against the heaviness of my eyelids.

11:56pm

I'm jolted awake by a loud

THUD THUD THUD THUD!

At first I'm **disoriented,** and then I remember where I am. In my luxury hotel room. I've fallen asleep on the sofa when I could be sleeping **diagonally** across my **PLUSH!** king-size mattress. What a waste!

The **BANGING** at the door continues.

It's probably Dad. Once before on holidays, he got locked outside our hotel room in the **NUDDY** when he mistook the exit for the bathroom door.

FLASHBACK

Bleary-eyed, I **shuffle** over to the hallway door.

I **PEER** through the peep-hole just to be certain it's Dad before opening up. I hope he's at least got **underwear** on this time!

180

I don't believe my eye. So I try the other one.
And I see the same UNBELIEVABLE sight.

The fish-eye lens of the peephole is DISTORTING the
face, but I would still recognise that chiselled jaw anywhere.
It can't be him though. It can't **actually** be ...

THE JUSTIN CHASE – International Recording Superstar and Teen Heart Throb!

He **BARGES** in, out of breath (and exceedingly handsome).

'PLEASE! YOU'VE GOTTA SAVE ME, BRO!' he pleads frantically.

He **SLAMS** the door shut behind him and hits the light switch, plunging us into **darkness**.

11:57pm

And if you thought WEDNESDAY was woeful,

just wait until ...

FUN FACTS

WITH JUSTIN CHASE

PARROTS don't have vocal chords, but they can **MIMIC** sounds, including human speech. Some parrots have learnt a vocabulary of over a thousand words!

Astronauts drink their **PEE**, but only once the urine has been recycled and filtered to make it drinkable.

Primates in the wild have been observed throwing rocks and sticks when threatened, but the HOWLER MONKEY does indeed throw its own **POO** as defence. Yikes!

Is that a dolphin or a shark **FIN** headed your way? **DOLPHIN** dorsal fins have a curve, whereas **SHARK** fins have a straight edge. Another big difference is dolphins are warm-blooded **mammals**, while sharks are cold-blooded **fish**.

S.O.S. is an AMBIGRAM. It reads the same right way up and upside down, which is useful for being spotted from the air. Other ambigrams are **dollop, pod** and **swims**.

But does **S.O.S.** stand for SAVE OUR SHIP or SAVE OUR SOULS? Originally, **neither!** It started out

purely as the most efficient **MORSE CODE** distress signal for ships in trouble. A continuous string of three dots – three dashes – three dots. The famous **ACRONYMS** came later.

HOW TO DRAW: NICKERS

STEP 1
Draw 2 circles next to each other.

STEP 2
Draw a dot in each circle and 3 strokes for eyelashes.

STEP 3
Draw a triangle with curved corners for the nose.

STEP 4
Draw a curve for a smile then a U & I for the tongue.

STEP 5
Draw a big upside down U for the face.

STEP 6
The ears are just like capital D's facing different directions.

STEP 7
Add two curved lines and a love heart for the collar.

STEP 8
Add the finishing touches. Muzzle: dots. Ears: strokes. Drool: optional. Add colour.

WOOF!*

*Great drawing, small human!

WHAT'S <u>YOUR</u> PREDICTION FOR THURSDAY?

_____

_____

_____

_____

_____

_____

_____

Draw an illustration of Thursday.

AND NOW ... A BRIEF MESSAGE FROM

EVA & MATT

SHE WROTE
THE WORDS

HE WROTE THE
OTHER WORDS
AND DREW THE
PICTURES

LITTLE
EVA:
Tropical
style →

← LITTLE
MATT:
Pirate
style

Hey there _____,

YOUR NAME HERE ↖ (Unless this is a library book. In that case,
just imagine your name here. Or use invisible ink).

YOU made it to Wednesday.* YAY! Thank you for sticking
with us to almost half-way through the WORST WEEK EVER!

We both love theme parks (do you?!), so we tried to make
this story a bit like a roller coaster ride by including:

a) laughs and thrills

b) unexpected twists

c) lots of screams

d) the possibility of spew

e) all of the above.

* Assuming you did actually get
through Monday and Tuesday
and didn't start straight on
Wednesday, which would be
a bit weird but is totally fine.
No judgement. Weird is good!

Speaking of wild rides, we're currently on one ourselves. Not literally – you're not allowed to bring your laptop on a big dipper! Figuratively. We are ecstatic, shaken and a little bit dizzy and it's all because of you. Yes, YOU!

YOU – the brilliant, incredibly good-looking reader with amazing taste in books. YOU could have picked any book from the shelf and YOU chose our silly book. And now, because of trend-setting YOU, WORST WEEK EVER is a worldwide hit being published all around the globe and being read by kids everywhere in lots of different languages!

We can't believe it. So THANK YOU! High fives and fist bumps. We can't wait to see where this ride takes us next.

Anyway, we hope you NEVER have a week like Justin's and may your undies always be sand-free! See you THURSDAY.

Best wishes,

Eva ♥ Matt ☺

P.S. Don't listen to Wolf Gruntz. DO NOT drink your pee!

P.P.S. Keep reading! The best way to try out lots of books is to be a member of your local library. Can you believe there are FREE books just waiting for you to borrow them? OK, so you do have to return them, but then you can borrow MORE free books! How amazing are libraries?! Answer: REALLY amazing!

P.P.P.S. Try to enjoy the ride! Even if it's a bit scary.

EVA AMORES is a designer/photographer who has worked for the Sydney Opera House and the ABC. She was born in the Philippines and moved to Australia during high school. She likes shoes, travelling and more shoes.

MATT COSGROVE is the best-selling author/illustrator of *Macca the Alpaca* and the *Epic Fail Tales* series. He was born and raised in western Sydney. He likes chocolate, avoiding social interactions and more chocolate.

Eva and Matt met when they were randomly placed together for a group assignment at university twenty-five years ago and they've been collaborating ever since. They've made dinner, cakes, a mess, the bed, mistakes, memories, poor fashion decisions and two actual humans, but this is their first book series together.

When they were in lockdown and the world felt a bit grim, they could have mastered sourdough or binge watched Netflix but, no, they decided to create this series instead - **THE WORST WEEK EVER!** (Sorry about that.)

Here's a photo of Eva and Matt so if you ever see them in real life you know to run in the opposite direction.

AS PIRATES
(in case they're in disguise)